# Learn to read with

# Posy the Pig

### Words by Sue Graves
### Illustrations by Jan Smith

INDEX

# "I'm going to a party!" said Posy the pig.

SiD PiGS PARTY!

This Saturday at 7 O'clock. Please come Posy and dance to the pop band M!G!

POSY

"I'll look like a pop star if I put on a wig."

The pink wig
didn't fit.
It was too big.

"This wig is
too big."

"I'm sure I'll find my green wig if I dig and dig."

The party was held in Sid Pig's rig.

For tea,
Posy ate a
big, ripe fig.

# After tea, all the pigs danced to a band called Mig.

# Then Posy won a prize for the best wig. She did a little jig.

"Your wig is the best!"

"Wow!" said
Posy. "What
a super gig!"

# The end